FUN READING ABOUT 【悦读中国】

CHINA

Science and Technology in Contemporary China

Gu Ming

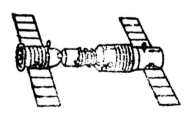

Huang Shan Publishing House

图书在版编目(CIP)数据

中国当代科技: 英文 / 顾鸣编著 ; 李国庆译.
-- 合肥 : 黄山书社, 2014.1
（悦读中国）
ISBN 978-7-5461-2021-8

Ⅰ. ①中… Ⅱ. ①顾… ②李… Ⅲ.
①科学技术－中国－通俗读物－英文 Ⅳ. ①N12-49

中国版本图书馆CIP数据核字(2013)第319401号

悦读中国：中国当代科技
YUE DU ZHONG GUO :ZHONG GUO DANG DAI KE JI

顾　鸣　编著

出 版 人：任耕耘
策　　划：任耕耘　蒋一谈
责任编辑：司　雯　李　南
责任印制：戚　帅　李　磊　　　　　　　　　　　　装帧设计：商子庄

出版发行：时代出版传媒股份有限公司（http://www.press-mart.com）
　　　　　黄山书社（http://www.hsbook.cn）
　　　　　官方直营书店网址（http://hsssbook.taobao.com）
　　　　　营销部电话：0551—63533762　63533768
　　　　　（合肥市政务文化新区翡翠路1118号出版传媒广场7层　邮编：230071）
经　　销：新华书店
印　　刷：安徽联众印刷有限公司

开本：710×875　1/16　　　　印张：6.25　　　　字数：80千字
版次：2014年4月第1版　　　　印次：2014年4月第1次印刷
书号：ISBN 978-7-5461-2021-8　　　　　　　　　定价：56.00元

Foreword

Science and technology is no longer limited to scientists. Seen everywhere, it has made life easier and the world comfortable to live in.

Science and technology has advanced rapidly in contemporary China, particularly over the past decades when Chinese government puts people's livelihood on top of its working list by introducing advanced technology in health care, environmental protection, energy conservation, emission reduction, prevention and reduction of natural disasters and the protection of public security. The advance has caught the world's eye made in the increase of rice yields by hybrid technology, and in the introduction of new energy resources like solar, wind, nuclear and biological, etc. The energy crisis that once threatened China is released. Also, fast progress is seen in the prevention and control technology against malaria, SARS virus, bird flu, etc. Today, science and technology has benefited us in every part of daily life.

Come with us for a trip to see some of China's contemporary scientific achievements and cutting-edge technology, to feel the power of science in this part of the world.

Contents

1 Information Technology

2 Medicine

3 Space Technology

4 New Energy Resources

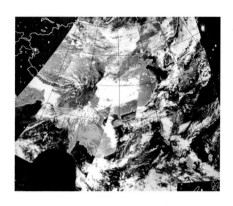

5 Oceans

6 Agriculture

7 Military Power

8 Mega Engineering Projects

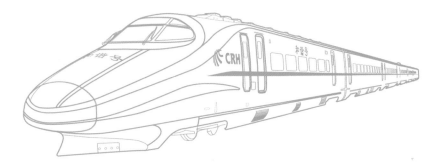

Information Technology

This world has become more informational than ever. The technology in computer science, network and communication has never been as influential as it is today. Presently, China's information industry has become a pillar industry, ranking the second in size worldwide. In some aspects, China is leading the world.

Tianhe-series Super Computers

170 black equipment cabinets lined up like soldiers in a powerful square team in a huge room inside the National University of Defense Technology—they are the Tianhe 2 super computer, a hundred percent self-designed and self-developed model.

Back to November 2009, its predecessor, Tianhe 1, also a self-developed model, won the first place for the fastest calculation in Asia by over one petaflops on an international competition for super computers. This speed marked China as the second country after the US capable of doing petaflops. This record lasted only a year, for in November 2010, Tianhe 1 broke its own record with 4.7 petaflops. The world was amazed at this "black horse" of China in computer technology. Liu Guangming, a member of the development team, simply said the following on the award issuing

◆ Tianhe 1 Super Computer

ceremony, "When a nation has worked hard day after day, night after night for 30 years on run, with only a 3-day break for Chinese New Year each year, hitting the first place in the world is a sure thing. "

◆ Tianhe 2 Super Computer

China didn't stop at this, for in June 2013, Tianhe 2 won the first place in the world again by peak 54.9 petaflops and 33.9 sustainable petaflops. It was indisputably the fastest computer worldwide.

Apart from Tianhe-series, China has other famous brands to boast of like *Shenwei*, *Shuguang* and *Shenteng*. After the US and Japan, China has become the third nation able to make and use one-gigaflop super commercial computers.

The Power of Tianhe Super Computers

In just one hour, Tianhe 2 is able to finish what 1.3 billion people can do for a thousand years, each having a calculator in hand. Tianhe's total storage capacity equals 60 billion books, each having 100 thousand characters in it.

Tianhe-series has exhibited its huge power in different aspects like spaceflight, aviation, energy resource exploration, weather forecast, medicine development, architectural design, finance and insurance. The aerodynamic configuration for a new model of airplane, for instance, used to take something between 3—5 years to complete. Now, with Tianhe 2, a dozen or so days are more than enough.

The Largest Internet in the World

Internet based on computers enables people to contact people anytime and anywhere in the world, to share joy, experience and help one another, disregard your ethnic group, nationality, age, gender, financial status and profession. With internet, you can pass knowledge or ideas. The earth has indeed become a "global village".

In this, China's internet is doubtlessly the largest in the world—not only in size, also in the number of netizens and areas. By June 30, 2013, China's netizens were as many as 591 million and the internet penetration, 44.1%. The momentum of progress is huge. For with the spreading 3G (the Third Generation Telecommunication) and wireless network, by the end of June 2013, mobile phone netizens were up to 464 million. In near future, China will be the largest market in the world for internet commerce and computer technology.

So far, China has many web portals like Sina, Tencent and Netease, social networking sites like Microblog and Renren, community forums like Skyline, Douban, and search engines like Baidu, Sogou and 360, needlessly to say QQ and Wechat for instant chatting. They have made life much easier for netizens.

◆ The 12th China Internet Conference, August 2013, Beijing

Part of the Internet Life for Chinese Netizens

Popular web portals:

 新浪网网址：http://www.sina.com

 网易网网址：http://www.163.com

鳳凰網 凤凰网网址：http://www.ifeng.com

Popular social network sites:

人人网 renren.com 人人网网址：http://www.renren.com

 新浪微博：http://weibo.com

Popular community forums:

豆瓣 douban 豆瓣网网址：http://www.douban.com

 天涯网网址：http://www.tianya.cn

Popular search sites:

Bai 百度 百度网网址：http://www.baidu.com

Popular chat tools:

 腾讯QQ 腾讯网网址：http://www.qq.com

International Standards for the Third Generation Mobile Communications

Mobile phones, a major instrument to get on the internet, are able to roam seamlessly from country to country, take photos, play music and videos, web surf and do e-commerce and teleconference. The Third Generation Telecommunication, commonly called 3G, has made all these possible.

As the largest mobile phone market on this globe, China has 1.1 billion mobile phone users. By the second season of 2013, 80.5 million of them went on internet via 3G mobile phones and the number was increasing.

International standards are necessary for 3G service and its data transmission speeds. So far, there are three: WCDMA, CDMA2000 and TD-SCDMA. Of the

◆ Passengers Surfing on Internet with Cell Phones on Subway Line Two, Shanghai

three, TD-SCDMA is a hundred percent Chinese design, and China has its proprietary intellectual property rights. In May 2000, the World Wireless Cable Association acknowledged TD-SCDMA, which marked China's leading position in mobile communication technology. Compared with others, TD-SCDMA has advantages: smaller radiation, more flexibility and low cost, which earned a reputation as "green 3G". Apart from the above mentioned, TD-SCDMA's TDD (Time Division Duplex) has been chosen by ITU (International Telecommunication Union) as the only technology to use. So far, this technology is still progressing.

Data

4G: A Wireless World Faster Than 3G

While people are enjoying the convenience of 3G, its next generation, 4G, is around the corner. By newer technology, 4G is faster and more efficient, 50 times faster than current 3G technology. You can imagine the feel in that lightening speed. Right now, the US, Europe, Japan and the ROK are busy working on it, but China is leading them all!

On the International Telecommunication Union conference held on January 18, 2012, China's TD-LTE and 3GPP's FDD-LTE from the European Standardization Organization are both made the 4G international standards, a proof to China's leading position in the world.

On December 4, 2013, Ministry of Industry and Information Technology of PRC issued business licenses to China Mobile, China Telecom and China Union for "LTE/fourth generation digital cellular mobile communication (TO-LTE)". This marked China's telecommunication industry into the 4G era.

◆ The 4G Library, Hubei Province

The Hubei new provincial library is fully covered by GSM, TD, WLAN and LTE, which enable people to get on the internet with CMCC-4G Wi-Fi signals via cell phones or laptops, into a transformed wireless network. Its download speed is up to 50M per second, ten times as fast as 3G. It is the same even in the remote corner of the library, more than good enough for on-line reading or video watching.

Medicine

● What Is Traditional Chinese Medicine?

A 3000 years old Chinese medicinal science, culturally different from Western medicine, it is based on a belief of both macroscopic and syndrome different treatments. Traditional Chinese medicine values prevention of disease and a long-term cultivation, both physical and mental. By this belief, one should start earlier, even before an illness actually happens and this is the fundamental difference from its Western counterpart.

● Are Modern Medicine in China and the Carry-on of Traditional Chinese Medicine the Same Thing?

Not really. Modern medicinal science in China has a wider coverage. It owes its remarkable achievements to traditional Chinese medicine, Western medicine and modern biology as well.

The Progress of Traditional Chinese Medicine Today

"I can be a volleyball attacker again," shouted in huge excitement by a member of Kazakhstan Science Academy after his annoying scapulohumeral periarthritis was cured in the Shanxi University of Traditional Chinese Medicine. On February 25, 2013, on a tour in China's Shanxi Province, he received acupuncture and cupping glass moxibustion treatment. The result was unbelievable, for in just half an hour he was able to lift his arm as much as he wanted. Two months later, he came again, this time, with his friend who had suffered scapulohumeral periarthritis for years.

To many, traditional Chinese medicine is magic, also mysterious. Simply by pressing on some acupoints and taking some ordinary items of food, one can get rid of an illness. This doubt is quite understandable. In the history of human science and technology, traditional Chinese medicine is the only something over 3000 years old and still in service. This is a miracle itself. Of recent years, ideas from traditional Chinese medicine like "naturopathy" and "prevention is more effective than medical treatment" have found more and more willing ears among Westerners. Many have come a long way to China studying traditional Chinese medicine. Food therapy, massage, acupuncture and *Guasha*, a popular treatment for sunstroke by scarping the patient, all being traditional Chinese regimens, have been seen across the globe. A famous German physicist, also a scholar in aerospace medicine and health engineering science exclaimed, "As a scientist, I know that traditional Chinese medicine is much easier than its Western counterpart in theory and fitness keeping, because the former comes from the origin of life while the latter focuses on the symptoms of human body. "

Of recent years, by combining traditional Chinese medicine, Western medicine and modern biology, new progress has happened: more treatment means from Western medicine are adopted and teams of both Chinese and Western medicinal doctors are

The Common Chinese Herbal Medicine

◆ Lotus Leaves

◆ Dandelion

◆ Mother Chrysanthemum

◆ Chinese Cinnamon

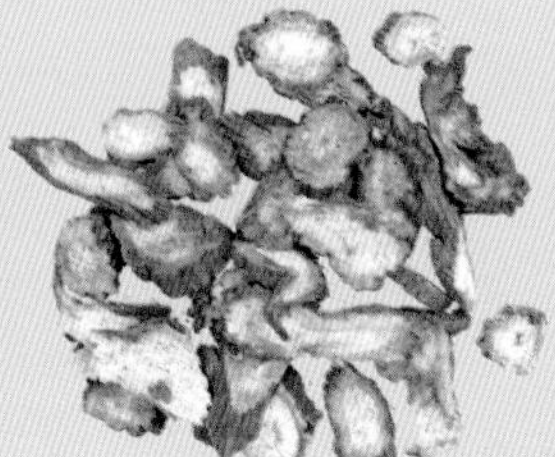

◆ Salvia Miltiorrhiza

◆ Motherwort

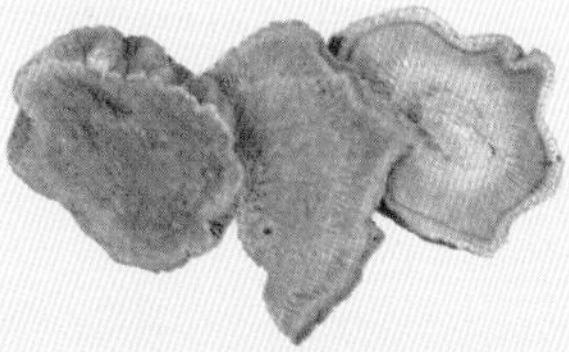

◆ Chinese Rhubarb

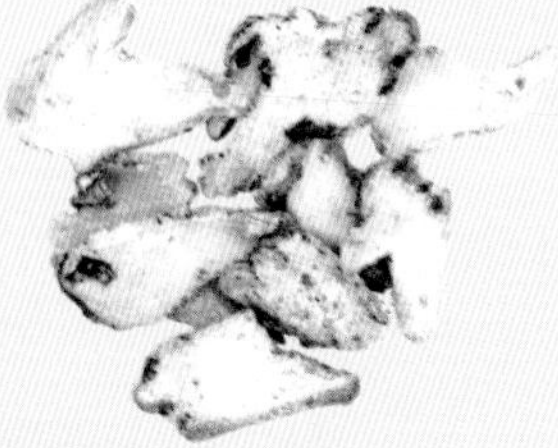

◆ Bletilla Striata

◆ Ganoderma Lucidum

founded to work on diseases like cardiovascular and cerebrovascular ones, cancers, diabetes mellitus, immune, digestive system, skin and endocrine dyscrasia problems. A treatment involving both traditional Chinese medicinal theory and Western medicinal treatment has worked very satisfactory, able to heal, more than just relieve pain. This has drawn a universal attention.

Traditional Chinese medicine research institutes have been founded in Japan and many Western countries. In 1991, a hospital of traditional Chinese medicine was founded in Germany; in 1995, the department of traditional Chinese medicine was founded in RMIT University, Australia. In 2013, the US Army hired traditional Chinese medicinal doctors to relieve pain and stress by acupuncture for some soldiers. For the first time, acupuncture was taken into the interdisciplinary study list for the US Army.

Difference Between Traditional Chinese and Western Medicines		
	Traditional Chinese medicine	Western medicine
Belief	Prevention comes before treatment	Treatment only
The way to diagnose	Look, listen, question and feel the pulse	Inquiry, echometer, X-ray machine and other apparatus
Treatments	Traditional Chinese medicine, prescriptions, qigong, acupuncture, scraping the patient and massage	Western medicine, muscle and intravenous shots, surgeries
Compositions of the medicine	From animals and plants	Chemicals
Concepts for keeping in good health	By intake of natural food, activities, balance of internal Yin and Yang	By supplement of vitamins and minerals to slow down metabolism

The Discovery of Artemisinin

Malaria is a deadly epidemic found in many countries. By a WHO report, every year about 200 million people get it and about a million die. The death toll list includes famous personages like Dante of famous Italian poet and Cromwell of British bourgeoisie revolution leader. Beginning from 1960s, developed countries like the US, France, Britain and Germany input a large amount of resources on the study of effective medicine against this deadly disease. No satisfactory progress was reported.

In February 1969, Chinese biologist Tu Youyou was entrusted with the task of developing an effective medicine against it. After numerous tests, in October 1971, she was finally able to extract artemisinin, a highly effective element from a Chinese medicinal herb called Artemisia annua. By 1978, all the 2099 malaria patients recovered after receiving artemisinin comprehensive treatment and this draw the world's eye. By 2005,

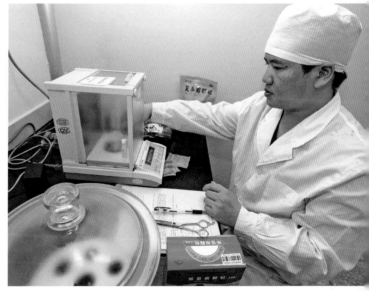

◆ Chinese Medicine Being Shipped to Africa
This medicine manufacturer in Liuzhou, Guangxi, is doing quality check before its product being shipped out. Its 400 thousand tons of yearly production of artemisinin is earmarked by the International Red Cross as the aid for African countries.

many countries established this treatment as number-one therapy for malaria patients. Numerous lives are brought back by this artemisinin treatment.

In September 2011, with this discovery, Tu Youyou received Lasker Medical Research Awards, the most renowned prize in the US medicinal industry. In her reward-winning speech, Tu Youyou said the following, "Ancient documents gave me aspirations whenever I met a dead end and I firmly believe traditional Chinese medicines make a treasure archive to be tapped for more effective medicines to benefit this contemporary world."

◆ Tu Youyou Receiving "Outstanding Contribution Award" from CACMS

Development of SARS Vaccine

Between November 2002 and August 2003, China as well as many nations was hit by an epidemic called SARS. In just one year, over 7000 Chinese people got it and over 800 died.

Chinese medical workers, apart from rescuing lives, immediately started developing SARS vaccine. Usually, such a process took at least a couple of years, but this time Chinese medicine workers had to race against time and they got to win. On December 5, 2004, inactivated vaccine, a hundred percent Chinese make, passed phase

◆ SARS Vaccine in Animal Experiment
On November 19, 2003, the inactivated vaccine for human SARS patients was born in the animal laboratory center of Wuhan University.

one test, which proved its safety and effectiveness. By people involved in this project, many times they had to work 20 hours a day and as soon as they entered their labs, drinking, eating and toileting became impossible for at least 6 hours.

It took much longer before it was ready on market. Even so, it proved SARS was preventable and curable before the power of Chinese medicinal research academies. So far, China has become the largest exporter of vaccines in the country. Among the latest on its product list is the vaccine for influenza type-A H1N1, a remarkable contribution for world's medicinal progress.

◆ Pupils at Siyang Town Primary School, Guangxi, Are Receiving Vaccination

Mouse Cloned by Chinese Scientists

Black hairs, sharp-pointed whiskers, a long tail and round eyes—it looks just like any other mouse but it is hugely different: it is the first cloned mouse called Xiaoxiao, or "tiny", in China, also the first one across the world by IPS stem cells. The success of Xiaoxiao proves that IPS technology is safe, making it possible to clone larger and adult mammals. As a new and finer way than the traditional, IPS is described by the *Times* as "one of the ten significant breakthroughs made in 2009 in medical science".

In July 2013, another mouse, Qingqing, was born, cloned from a black rat's lung cells by the scientists of Peking University. This is another significant step China made in clone technology and regenerative medical science.

Chinese scientists are working on the possibility of creating stem cells

Chronicles

1979: The first crucian about 8 cm long was born by blastula stage technology in Wuhan Aquatic Organism of Chinese Academy of Sciences.

1999: By early panda embryos cloned from the eggs of rabbits, Chinese scientists proved the possibility of clone technology for the sake of preservation of highly endangered wildlife species.

June 2000: Two goats were born by somatic cell cloning in China's Northwest Agriculture & Forestry University. One died early.

March 2012: The first baby bull, about 58.2 kilograms, was born by clone technology in Chinese Academy of Agricultural Sciences. It is the first time zona pellucid technology was applied in China.

on human bodies. The promise is good. In near future, many incurable illnesses today like thalassemia, Parkinson's disease and diabetes will be curable.

◆ The Birth of China's First Allosome Cloned Goat
A baby lamb was born on January 21, 2004, 132 days after embryo transplantation from a somatic cell of an ibex and an ovocyte from a goat into a rutting goat mother.

Space Technology

China is the fifth nation in the world able to develop and launch man-made earth satellites.

China is the third nation in the world able to develop and launch return satellites.

China is the fifth country in the world able to launch lunar probes.

China is the third country in the world able to do manned space flights.

Man-made Satellites

Satellites are bodies that move around planets. The moon that orbits around the earth is one. Man-made satellites, as the name suggests, are industrial products of man, to gather weather information, guide airplanes, detect earth resources and do military missions.

In this, China space technology was a later comer—by developing man-made satellites in late 1950s, when the Soviet Union and the United States had already sent theirs into space. On April 24, 1970, the first China made, Dongfanghong 1, was up, sending the melody of *The East is Red* back to the earth, and ranking China as the fifth

Model of Dongfanghong 1

Four Major Space
Centers of China

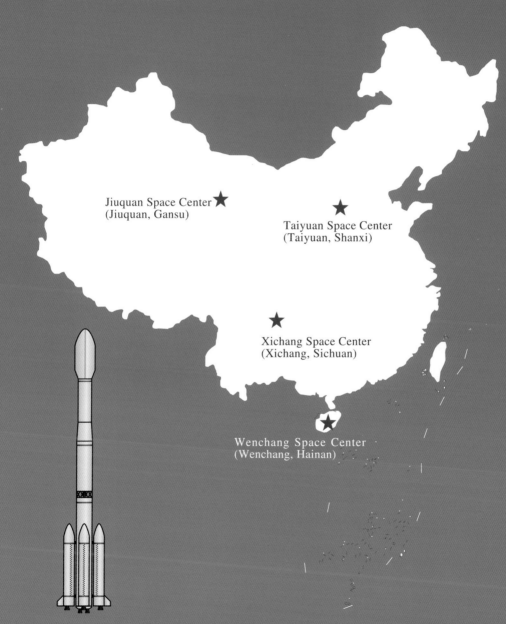

Jiuquan Space Center
(Jiuquan, Gansu)

Taiyuan Space Center
(Taiyuan, Shanxi)

Xichang Space Center
(Xichang, Sichuan)

Wenchang Space Center
(Wenchang, Hainan)

nation in this field. Since then, China has managed to keep abreast with the advance of the world. By now, China has dozens of man-made satellites on orbits.

Data

Looking for Intelligent Beings in Outer Space

Man, tremendously fascinated by the reports of UFO, has never ceased his efforts looking for intelligent beings in outer space. A fine example is the Hollywood movie *E.T.* Man-made satellites make a fine instrument to send signals to intelligent beings if there are any. Man-made satellite "Traveler" has broadcasted greetings from man into deep space in sixty languages. Singing from a Peking Opera, *Ode to Joy* by Beethoven, as well as photos of a Chinese family dinner table and the Great Wall were sent.

Shenzhou Spacecrafts

Everyone has a dream about the outer space and everyone wants, if opportunity avails, to see it. Today, astronauts from the US, Russia and China have done it. Yet this is only the first step man made to gain knowledge about and to tap space resources.

Shenzhou is the name for Chinese spacecrafts. Some of its functions outdo the spacecrafts from other nations. On November 20, 1999, Shenzhou 1 was launched into its orbit. On June 13, 2013, Shenzhou 10 successfully docked to Tiangong 1 and this marked a giant step China made in manned spacecraft engineering. During the 15 days

◆ Shenzhou 10 Successfully Docked to Tiangong 1

◆ Wang Yaping Is Lecturing from Space

in space, three Chinese astronauts, for the first time, lectured to children back on the earth. This class was warmly received by children and adults alike. Numerous people were engrossed before TV sets. Wang Yaping, the female astronaut, was the primary lecturer. She showed a wonderful zero gravity world in which ordinary objects around us like simple pendulum ball, spinning top and water film became extraordinary.

Different Properties Displayed on the Earth and in Space

Small Ball Simple Pendulum Test	Spinning Top Turning Test
A small metal ball tied by a rope to a T-shaped stand is lifted to a height before let go.	Give a gentle push to the spinning top while it is turning.

On the earth: Repeated simple pendulum motions.

On the earth: The spinning top will down and slowly stops its motion.

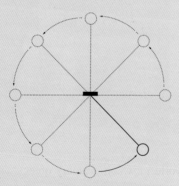

In space: Circling motions around the stand.

In space: The spinning top will continue rotating in its axial direction.

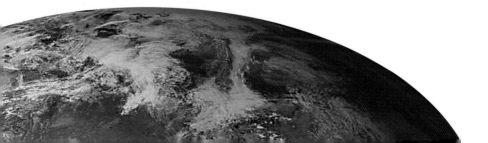

Changzheng-series Carrier Rockets

How do they send man-made satellites or manned spacecrafts up into space?

Carrier rockets may send, apart from man-made satellites and manned spacecrafts, spaceport and space probes too, into their designated orbits.

Up to now, China has developed 12 models in Changzheng-series. By June 11, 2013, of the 177 blast-off, 169 are successful. Sending a rocket onto its designated orbit is just like hitting a bull's eye with a bullet and you can imagine the difficulty. Changzheng 5 being developed is super powerful, up to 240 tons of thrust and its main performance indexes are leading in the world.

High-performance, low cost, bigger thrust, pollution free and re-useable, these are the objectives pursued by different countries including China.

◆ The Blast-off of Changzheng 2, the Carrier for Shenzhou 10 on June 11 , 2013

◆ Astronauts on Shenzhou 10

◆ The Astronauts of Shenzhou 10 and Their Re-entry Capsule

China's Lunar Exploration Program

The moon, our nearest neighbor, is closer to us than any other celestial body. Even in ancient history, man tried to make exploratory efforts. In 1959, the Soviet Union successfully sent Moon 1 and in 1969, US astronauts set their feet in the moon, and this marked a new episode in man's space exploration.

Even in ancient antiquity, Chinese people enjoyed a tale of a young lady who managed to fly up to the moon. It had been an unfulfilled dream to Chinese nation for millenniums. In 2004, China's lunar exploration program named Chang'e Project started. So far, China has sent, respectively in October 2007 and October 2010, Chang'e 1 and Chang'e 2 into their lunar orbits, to do a circumlunar flight and a controlled collision. They have sent back much information, including videos and data about the moon.

On December 2, 2013, China sent Chang'e 3 lunar probe to the moon. It carried a lunar vehicle, a near ultraviolet telescope, cameras and radars. For the first time, China's soft landing on the moon was obtained, to be followed by a 90-day unmanned exploration and survival of moon nights. This is a preparation for astronauts walking on the moon.

◆ Exhibition About the Moon, Held Inside Beijing
Science and Technology Museum
In August 2013, a museum about the moon was open
in Beijing Science and Technology Museum for
young people.

High-intelligence Robot: Rover Jade Hare, China's Lunar Vehicle

The rover Chang'e 3 carried was named Jade Hare, a high-intelligence robot able to function in different environments. It navigates by itself and is able to avoid obstacles. While moving, it detects mineral compositions on the moon and its structural change below the moon surface.

The survival of this rover on the moon is a mountainous task. It has to endure abrupt temperature change, up to 127℃ during the day and minus 183℃ at night. Its electronic parts must be able to work properly in this extreme situation.

At an hourly speed up to 200 meters, it can walk for 10 kilograms at one go. During its 3-month life expectancy, it is able to do 3-D videos, infrared spectroscopic analysis and determination of the lunar soil thickness and structure. Data from an on-site analysis will be sent back.

◆ Jade Hare, a Product of China's Independent Research and Development, Is on Display on an International Exhibition

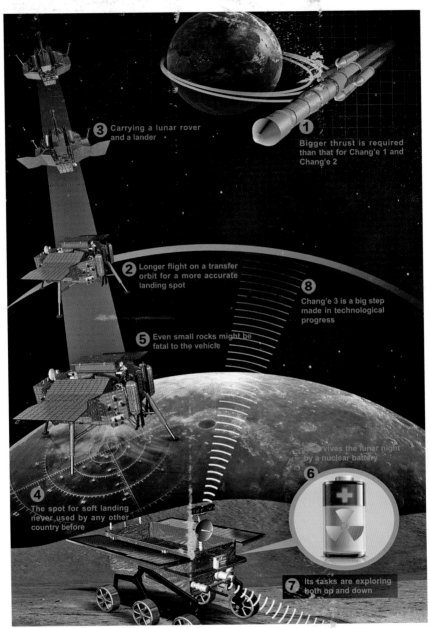

◆ The Mission from Beginning to the End

New Energy Resources

Energy resources are consumed even faster in the 21st century, while the deposits of fossil oil, coal and natural gas are fast diminishing. New energy resources are badly needed. China has made efforts in recent years by tapping rural biogas and nuclear energy, even more so, on the use of energy from solar, wind, water, plant and geothermal resources.

The Use of Marsh Gas in Countryside

You may wonder in Chinese countryside: there is no natural gas but people can cook with a gas stove; no electricity but people have lights in the evening. Why? It is because many Chinese households in countryside have a methane generating pit in backyard.

What is marsh gas, anyway? It is a flammable gas, a renewable energy source often found in a wetland, a sink or a manure pit. China probably has more methane-generating pits than any other nation in the world and its number has kept growing. By the end of

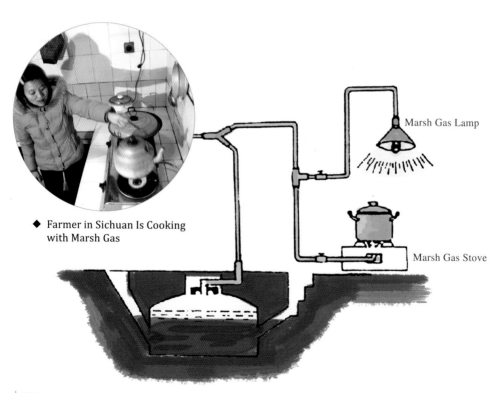

Marsh Gas Lamp

Marsh Gas Stove

◆ Farmer in Sichuan Is Cooking with Marsh Gas

◆ Nanyang Biological Marsh Gas Project, the Largest of Its Kind in the World
This project has 26 world largest fermentation cylinders. Put together, they are able to produce half a million cubic meters of marsh gas a day. This project has cut the yearly consumption of coal by 120 thousand tons, underground water by 3 million tons, emission of carbon dioxide by 1.1 million tons and sulfur dioxide by 33.1 thousand tons.

2010, over 40 million households in China's countryside have one.

"You need no firewood, no coal when you cook. All you need is turn it on, just like city people do in their kitchens." Zhao Ailan, a farmer in Shandong, said the above. She just had a pit built next to the house.

It was slow at beginning, but as soon as governmental workers explained how marsh gas worked, farmers rushed for it. A pit about 10 square meters large takes nothing more than the faeces from four pigs, which is enough for the lighting and cooking for a family of four. To a farmer in China, keeping four pigs is nothing. More than the dung from four hogs, you get organic manure as well, which is pollution-free, drought resisting and anti-freezing to drops. A marsh gas generating pit keeps environments clean and improves sanitary conditions.

Data

Straw Gasification

Over recent years, in China's countryside, a new energy resource is developed, straw gasification. Straw from crops is much, and by gasification inside a furnace it produces flammable gas for households to use, either for cooking or for heating.

Straw gasification is more advantageous than marsh gas, for it is not bound by a certain type of weather, particularly good in China's north, where it is often

◆ Worker at a Village Straw Gasification Workshop in Liaocheng, Shandong Province
This one-thousand-stere straw gasification station of 1.8 million Yuan investment completed in November 2012 in Yuji Village of Liaocheng, Shandong Province consumes 450 kilograms of straw each day, able to provide fuel to all the 626 households for cooking. Villagers trade 1 kilogram of straw of wheat, corn or corncob for 2 cubic meters of gas.

freezing cold. Also, straw has many varieties like wheat, corn, sorghum, rice, cavings, tree branches, saw dust and weed. Some trash from daily life is also usable.

Straw gasification takes village as a unit. One engineering project is able to serve several hundred households. You simply turn on the gas at home to cook.

By Chen Luqin, a farmer in Dabeiguan Village of Hebei Province, it costs them only 216 Yuan for a yearly use of straw gasification, but 480 if they use liquefied gas. Straw gasification is indeed inexpensive, clean and convenient.

The Largest Nuclear Power Unit in the World Under Construction

CCTV, China Central Television, broadcast alive to the world at 9:50 on January 29, 2013, the successful installation of an 830-ton part, the AP1000 containment's cover head in Number One Nuclear Islet of Sanmen County, Zhejiang Province by workers with a crawler-type crane. With this, this nuclear power station received its last protective screen against nuclear leaks. This marked China's leading

◆ Daya Bay Nuclear Power Plant
This plant, the second China ever had on its mainland but the first for commercial use, is on the Dapeng Peninsular of Shenzhen, Guangdong Province. In 2012, its total generating capacity was up to 261.3 billion kilowatt-hour. This means the reduction of coal consumption by 20.6 million tons, carbon dioxide release by 36.19 million tons, sulfur dioxide release by 0.35 million tons and nitrogen oxide emission by 0.23 million tons.

◆ The Control Center of Qinshan Nuclear Power Plant
In China's Haiyan County of Zhejiang Province, Qinshan Nuclear Power Plant is China's first self designed, built and managed pressurized water nuclear power station on 0.3 million kilowatts level. Up to now, it has kept a record of 20-year safe production.

position in nuclear technology.

Nuclear energy for electricity generation produces no greenhouse gases. Nuclear energy is inexpensive and powerful, easy to be stored and transmitted and because of this, nuclear energy has had dynamic progress across the world. It is also the orientation for China in its electricity structural adjustment.

By the end of July 2013, China has five large nuclear power stations completed, 17 power units in function, all having kept a very satisfactory safety records. Additionally 29 units are being built, to rank China the first in number once they are completed. By a governmental plan, by the year of 2020, nuclear power will take 5 percent of China's total electricity generated.

Jiuquan Wind Power Base, the Largest in the World

China's vast territory has a huge resource of wind power. Beginning from 1990s, China has boosted wind power electricity generation and by the end of 2009, its total installation capacity has surpassed that of the US to become the largest in the world and the growth has been fast. In 2012, the total generating capacity by wind power was100.8 billion kilowatt-hour, enough for 40 million households to use. Wind power, after thermal and hydro, has become the third largest source for electricity generation in China.

◆ The Wind Power Base in Jiuquan, Gansu Province

◆ The Off-shore Wind Power Plant by the East Sea Bridge
Each barrel of the windmill is 92 meters tall, about the height of a 30-story building. Each blade is 45 meters long.

Large groups of windmills in silver white color are seen lining up the road from Dunhuang to Jiayuguan Pass in China's Gansu Province. Their huge blades are turning in wind, making a fascinating landscape. These windmills belong to Jiuquan Wind Power Base of Gansu Province, the largest wind power base in the world.

Jiuquan of Gansu Province, with a gross reserve of 150 million kilowatts, has more wind power resource than anywhere in China. Its Guazhou area is called "the wind bank". By local people, Guazhou has just one wind in a year, but it lasts from spring to winter. The construction of wind power bases in Guazhou began in 1996. By now, Guazhou has 32 large wind power plants, generating in total 6 billion kilowatt-hour a year, which means the decrease in the use of coal by 2 million tons and the emission of carbon dioxide by 4.8 million tons a year.

Of recent years, off-shore wind power projects have gained a fast progress. Apart from Europe, in November 2010, China had in Shanghai the only off-shore wind plant in the world, which is able to generate on-grid 100 thousand kilowatts, enough for 200 thousand households to use for a year.

Data

The low-carbon Awareness Among Chinese People

With the fast progress of energy conservation and environment protection, Chinese people's low-carbon awareness has become strong. People have replaced plastic bags with environmental friendly ones. They have reduced the use of disposable chopsticks and toothbrushes. They have become economical in using water and paper. Many people have replaced electricity consuming incandescent light bulbs with energy saving LED. And many people have turned to automobiles with a smaller output volume. These efforts have paid off, for the country has become cleaner.

◆ **Environmental Friendly Tableware Made with Ecological Oddments**
A Shandong company successfully invented tableware in April 2011 with bagasse and straw. It is very environmental friendly, recyclable and is able to degrade to become organic manure for crops. Its yearly production is about 1.92 billion sets, exported to the US, Japan and ROK.

◆ **Low-carbon and Environmental Friendly Bicycle Group Weddings Held in Harbin, Heilongjiang Province in September 2013**

The Largest Solar Energy Industry in the World

A couple of residents are excitedly trying newly installed lighting system on their corridors. With the sound of footsteps, it is on; with the dying sound of footsteps, it is off—all being automatic. This neighborhood is old, having had no lighting system on corridors for years. In August 2013, it was changed, for a new type of lighting system using solar capacity energy storage was installed. It stores solar energy during the day and starts to work at night, triggered by a sound operated switch. It is a big help to the residents.

Solar energy is nothing new in daily life. With more and more attention given by the government, China has become the largest manufacturer in the world of photovoltaic modules. Solar cells for example, which have been widely used in spaceports, automobiles, airplanes and LED. Just in the first half of 2013, the quantity of solar cells exported from China was up to 250 million. So far, solar energy is used in many aspects of life, taking a shower, lighting, water boiling, cooking, heating, telecommunicating, broadcasting and irrigating fields. Solar

◆ Solar-energy Trash Cans Used in Handan, Hebei Province

Along the Xuechi Road of Handan are dozens of trash cans using solar energy. Their solar energy panels on top can light up a LED energy saving lamp for five hours at night.

◆ **Solar Energy Automobile, Made by a Senior High School Student in Zhejiang Province**
Zhu Zhenlin successfully made a solar-energy automobile in April 2012, at the cost of 15 thousand RMB. This 3.2 meters long and 1.4 meters tall vehicle has everything needed, accelerator, brake, steering wheel, turn lights and rearview mirrors. On top of the vehicle are 22 solar energy panels and in its trunk are 6 12V batteries. Left in sunshine for 4 hours, it is able to run 70 kilometers.

energy water heaters and cookers are popular.

In terms of solar energy, Qinghai and Tibet have more resources than any other in China. A solar cooker with just 2 square meters day-lighting area works just like a 2000-watt electricity stove, enough to boil water, stir-fry food and cook rice. Every stove like this means a 1000 square meters large pasture is spared. Apart from cooking, solar energy is used for electricity generation. So far, solar energy has provided electricity to

160 thousand households in Inner Mongolia, Xinjiang, Gansu, Qinghai and Sichuan.

Apart from lighting, in Qinghai-Tibet Plateau, people have promoted solar greenhouse technology. In the old days, all vegetables and fruits were shipped in by air. Now, with solar greenhouses available, fresh vegetables, fruits, meat and eggs are available throughout a year.

◆ Solar-energy Insect Killing Lamps Used in Countryside of Wuxi, Jiangsu Province
Many paddy fields in Wuxi, Jiangsu Province have a unique insect killing lamp powered by electricity from solar energy. By a 365 nm wave length, it lures and kills insects.

Oceans

Oceans are indeed treasure troves to mankind, for they make a food resource one thousand times bigger than the crops from lands, all put together. Yet people have known very little about oceans, not more than five percent of the knowledge about them, even man has made huge efforts in doing so. Over a million, or 50 million species by estimation, have remained unknown to mankind. China has made great efforts to remedy this situation.

Deep-sea Manned Submersible
Jiaolong

Chinese nation completed two almost impossible missions in June 2012. One is the flight to the moon, and another, a deep-sea dive accomplished by submersible *Jiaolong*. Scientists from 7000 meters below sea surface and in space 343 kilometers from the earth greeted one another.

After the US, France, Russia and Japan, China became the fifth nation able to do manned deep-sea diving and *Jiaolong* was the first operational instrument China ever had, self designed, developed and made.

June 27, 2012 was unforgettable. On that day *Jiaolong* set a record by diving

Maximum Depth Different Nations Reached with Manned Submersibles	
"Trieste", US	10916 meters deep (exploring)
"Deep Sea Challenger", US	10898 meters deep (exploring)
"Alvin", US	4500 meters deep (operational)
"*Jiaolong*", China	7062 meters deep (operational)
"Deep Sea 6500", Japan	6527 meters deep (operational)
"Peace-I", Russia	6000 meters deep (operational)
"Nautilus", France	6000 meters deep (operational)

◆ Deep-sea Manned Submersible *Jiaolong*

◆ Photos *Jiaolong* Took at the Bottom of an Ocean 5000 Meters Below Surface

7062.68 meters below surface in the Mariana Trench in West Pacific. It collected samples of sediment and minerals, as well as living species by baiting.

On September 19, 2013, *Jiaolong* docked to its mother port after its 103-day long mission completed, during which time it carried 10 scientists down to the bottom of the ocean on 22 times of diving. They collected 71 kinds of living creatures, 161 shells cores, 8 shells, 32 rocks and 180 kilograms of deposited sediment. To sample collection in oceanic studies, this mission was hugely significant. By Ye Cong, a deep sea diver on board, *Jiaolong* was able to work like a taxi in deep water. It was an edged tool for deep sea operations like bottom development, salvage and life saving.

HY-2 Ocean-watching Satellite

China needed satellites to observe and administrate its 3 million square kilometers sea area and HY-2 was just for the purpose. Like a huge net, the observation covers everything that happens in the sea, even a plastic bottle floating on water.

So far, China has launched three ocean-watching satellites, all being independently designed and developed, all being internationally advanced in technology. HY-2 launched in August 2011 was the first for dynamic environments, able to work all weather around the clock to gather information about wind field, waves, currents, tides and surface temperature. It can provide real-time information and warn before a

◆ The Blast-off of HY-2 Satellite

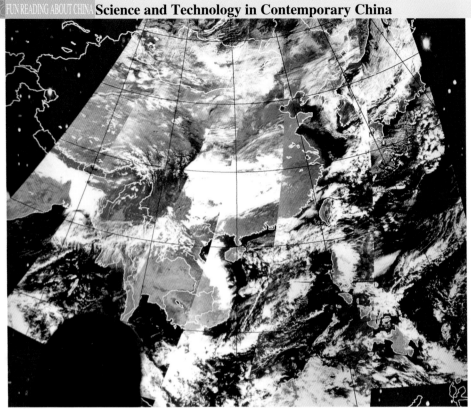

◆ Meteorological Chart from the Satellite

disaster happens. It is the only microwave remote sensing satellite moving on its orbit in the world able to do it. Since it began functioning, it has accurately and repeatedly predicted the coming of typhoons, a great help to China's deep-sea fishing industry. The information it provided helped the success of launch for Shenzhou 9 manned spacecraft. It also helps the studies of Nino phenomenon and global warming.

Fresh Water from the Sea

Workers are drinking fresh water desalinated from sea water on the first phase of this project, Beijiang Electricity Generation Plant of Tianjin. The fresh water desalinated is potable. After it is connected to the water supply system, it will provide 200 thousand tons of fresh water each day to the city.

Sea water takes up 97.2 percent of all the water on this globe but it is not drinkable. What a waste, when fresh water resource is fast diminishing. So people have turned eyes to sea water desalination technology. In 10 years, when daily capacity is up to 1.7 million tons, it will tremendously ease the fresh water shortage China is suffering now.

Sea water desalination, usually, is conducted in two ways: by distillation and by

◆ Sea Water Desalination Workshop in Qingdao, Shandong Province

◆ The Production Line for Bottled Desalinated Sea Water

reverse osmosis process. Distillation as a mature technology costs much energy, while the low-cost reverse osmosis process, over the past ten years, has been fast developing. As the fourth nation in the world who has the technical knowhow, by the end of 2012, China had processed sea water 700 thousand tons per day and its industrialization is coming.

Jiangxia Tidal Energy Power Plant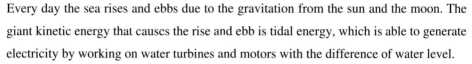

Every day the sea rises and ebbs due to the gravitation from the sun and the moon. The giant kinetic energy that causes the rise and ebb is tidal energy, which is able to generate electricity by working on water turbines and motors with the difference of water level.

Southeastern China has a zigzagging coastal line about 18 thousand kilometers long, a huge "bank" for tidal energy. Ever since 1980s, a group of tidal energy power plants have been built, and among them, Jiangxia Tidal Energy Power Plant in Wenling County of Zhejiang Province is the largest, not only in China, but also in Asia. Even in the world it ranks the third in size. Combined into the grid in May 1980, it is able to function both when the sea rises and ebbs. Leading in technology, it generates averagely 7.2 million kilowatt-hour a year.

So far, the higher cost is the bottleneck for the popularity of tidal power generation and this is also the reason Jiangxia is still in its experimental phase. The time for this kind of energy is about to come and the operation of Jiangxia, as well as the technology it has applied, makes the preparation for newer models of bigger capacity to be used in future.

In 2013, Wenzhou started a program to tap ocean energy. By it, the total capacity of tidal energy power to be generated is 0.4 million kilowatts ranking the first in the world.

◆ Jiangxia Tidal Energy Power Plant
In the first half of 2013, Jiangxia Tidal Energy Power Plant generated electricity up to 3.8 million kilowatt-hour, 0.291 million kilowatt-hour more on year-on-year basis. It was the highest output in its 30-year history.

6

Agriculture

China is a big agricultural country and farming has been its pillar economy for several thousand years. After the founding of New China, with ongoing agricultural modernization, farming technology has gained a rapid progress as seen in hybrid rice and transgenic wheat, etc. Not only solving the food and clothing problem for Chinese nation, the progress has also relieved food shortage in the world.

Oriental Magic Rice

China had a severe food shortage around 1960s, when the rice yield for a *Mu* was less than 300 kilos. The natural disasters for years running made the situation even worse. People were hungry. Having enough food was the biggest wish for everyone.

Today, food shortage no longer exists and China is self-sufficient in grain production. The credit goes to a significant invention: hybrid rice.

After years of hard work, in 1973, scientist Yuan Longping worked out a hybrid rice variety, yielding averagely 20 percent more from per-unit area than before. Yuan

◆ Farmers in Anhui Province Are Harvesting Hybrid Rice

◆ Yuan Longping, Father of Hybrid Rice

Longping didn't stop, for in September 2011, a newer variety even higher in yield came, averagely 900 kilos per *Mu*. This super rice is not only high in yield; it is also on the first or the second class quality by government standards. The promotion of this variety to 100 million *Mu* brings 15 billion kilos more rice, enough to feed 40 million people. To Yuan Longping, this is still not enough, for he and his team are working on the fourth generation of that variety.

The US is earlier in developing hybrid rice. When Yuan Longping's variety was introduced into the US for the first time, their scientists were taken aback by this magic variety from the East. So far, over 30 countries have introduced this variety. The result has been very encouraging; the population of hungry people has been reduced from 50 percent from mid 20th century to now only 20 percent. Yuan Longping, the one who made this happen, is duly described as "father of hybrid rice".

What Is "Hybrid Rice" Any Way?

It is a new variety through hybridization from two different in inheritance. The new variety will carry on good properties of each. Usually, a hybrid rice variety grows better, having bigger ears and bigger grains and stress-resistance. It is a higher-yield variety.

"Fathers" of Hybrid Rice		
The US	Henry Beachell	The first one in the world who advanced the theory and technology, successful in experiments in 1963. As the "father of hybrid rice", he won the World Food Prize in 1996. His technology, due to some inherent defect however, failed to be applied on a large scale.
China	Yuan Longping	Yuan Longping began the research of hybrid rice technology from 1964 and achieved the first success in 1975. In 1995, he initiated a newer variety and in 1997, drew the technical map for "super hybrid rice". He has broken the bottleneck for the popularization of hybrid rice.

Transgenosis Insect-resistant Cotton

Cotton farming was severely hit in 1990s in China, when cotton bollworms destroyed numerous crops. As the largest cotton producer in the world, China's economy suffered a severe loss.

Because of this, Chinese government strengthened its efforts in scientific research for cotton farming. In 1993, after transplanting insect killing genes China got a brand new variety, to be the second nation in the world who could do this. Several hundred varieties of insect-resistant cotton have received "safety certificate" in China. In January 2002, SGK321, after going through a tough evaluation, became the first in the world bivalent transgenosis insect resistant breed.

95 percent of cottons in China are transgenosis. In the old days, a crop needed 15 spreads of pesticide, now, just ten. Over the past 20 years, Chinese cotton farmers have been spared of harm from cotton bollworms.

Apart from insect-resistance, there are other aspects transgenosis technology is applied. Prof. Chen Xiaoya and his team developed a way for cotton fibers to

◆ China's Transgenosis Insect-resistant Cotton

accept keratin from rabbits and sheep. The new variety is bright, soft, more warmth-keeping and elastic. They have taken out patent for this technology.

◆ Farmers in Gansu Province Harvesting Cotton

Agrotechnical Stations

In hot summer sunshine, a worker from local agrotechnical station is tutoring to a farmer about how to graft watermelons. By the worker, grafting by this new technology will increase the yield by at least 20% and it has another benefit: more resistant to diseases like blight.

Almost every area on county level in China has a station like this, which introduces science and technology to farmers.

These agricultural technical station workers have a nickname: mud-coated legs

◆ Agrotechnical Station Worker in Yibin,Sichuan Province Is Teaching New Technology to Farmers

because they stand in field with farmers while doing their job. Teaching new technology is only part of their work, for they keep close watch at the situation of harmful insects, summarize experience and make suggestions, promote new technology and do exchange programs with other places, even foreign countries. Thanks to their work, agriculture in China has made a huge progress on the road of modernization.

◆ Long-stem Gourd, New Calabash Variety Developed by Guangdong Foshan Agricultural Science Academy

Military Power

China is the fifth nation in the world able to make a nuclear strike from underwater.

China is the tenth nation having an aircraft carrier.

China has armed its military forces with high-power laser technology, which is able to instantly destroy a missile from invaders.

China has mastered the technical knowhow for aircraft's small momentum orbital transfer technology, which is able to alter the orbit at will for a missile, making it impossible to be intercepted.

China has mastered for its submarines the super quite technology unable to be detected by any device so far.

China's Powerful Land Army

"Never fight Chinese army on land," British marshal Montgomery said on a reception party in his honor by his Chinese host in 1960, "this is my advice to any military leader. Whoever does it will be bogged in China."

A US army general said a similar thing, "Fighting Chinese land army is just like fighting the fear deep in one's heart. It is an intrinsic fear not to be conquered by any force."

On the National Day military parade of 2013, China once again showed its military muscles. Its land army has 1.7 million people in active and 0.8 million in reserve

◆ PLA's Guard of Honor

◆ Antiaircraft Missile Force in the National Day Military Parade

service. It has 7000 main battle tanks, 2200 infantry fighting vehicles, 5500 armored personal carriers and 25 thousand pieces of artillery, antiaircraft artillery included.

With the ongoing progress of modern mechanization and digitalization, Chinese land army has gained sophisticated sci-tech power, the most sophisticated in the world. In chemical defense, disinfection, electronic and information countermeasures and tactic missile making, China is leading in the world.

Ballistic Missile Nuclear Submarines

So far, man has made 180 ballistic missile nuclear submarines worldwide and 60 of them are in service. The first China made by independent efforts is called "092 ballistic missile nuclear submarine", which successfully launched a ballistic missile in September 1988, uttering China into the club of five after the US, U.K, Russia and France able to do nuclear strike from underwater. The "096 model" being developed is even more powerful, and it has made a technical breakthrough in noiselessness and invisibility.

Ballistic missile nuclear submarines are also called "strategic missile nuclear submarine", which are able to launch trans-continental missiles. They are more invisible and mobile, safer and super powerful. They are the main combat force for the 21st century and the use of them will bring immeasurable damage to mankind. A single warhead from a missile is enough to wipe a city off the map. In 1964, right after the first nuclear test, China announced to the world, "At any time and in any circumstances, China will not be the first to use nuclear weapons."

◆ Chinese Navy's Ballistic Missile Nuclear Submarine

Data

Liaoning Aircraft Carrier

In September 2013, Liaoning Aircraft Carrier finished tests of fighters' continuous landing and takeoff, flight to and back to the carrier, short-range ski-jump takeoff, etc. These tests marked the initial fighting ability. On November 28, 2013, Liaoning Aircraft Carrier traveled through the Taiwan Straight to China's South Sea for more tests and training.

As the first carrier for fixed-wing aircrafts, Liaoning Aircraft Carrier started service in China's Navy in September 2012. In near future, aircrafts built by Chinese people will be seen in oceans.

◆ Liaoning Aircraft Carrier

Yilong UAV

As its name suggests, UAV is unmanned aerial vehicle for a military mission. The models China has developed in recent years like *Yilong*, *Tianyi*, *Lanhu* and *Yeying*, have drawn the world's eye for their widely acknowledged sophistication and multipurpose capability. Among them, the *Yilong* can do a precise strike and long distance and long-time stealthy reconnoiter tasks without being discovered.

  Yilong is for both military and civilian use. Its beautiful body and 14-meter wings have won it a nickname "phantom in the air". It can monitor, scout and strike. Its video, infrared and laser capability make it a hunting bird gliding in the sky, able to detect any target in an area 4000 kilometers across. It can track and destroy a target at 120

◆ Yilong UAV

kilometers per hour in a mute state. It is very good for civilian missions like disaster surveillance, environmental protection, drug smuggling control, weather observation, geological exploration, land surveying and forestry fire hazard detection.

8

Mega Engineering Projects

The longest high speed one in the world: Beijing-Shanghai High-speed Railway.

The longest cross-sea bridge in the world: Hangzhou Bay Bridge.

The largest network of highways in the world: Five north-south ones and seven east-west ones.

The largest water conservancy project in the world: South-water-to-north Project.

The largest electricity engineering project: Western-electricity-to-east Project.

The largest single-structure in the world: Terminal Three of the Capital International Airport.

The highest-altitude railway in the world: Qinghai-Tibet Railway.

The largest hydropower station in the world: The Three Gorges Hydroelectric Power Station.

The largest marine-reclamation land project: Lingang New Town, Shanghai.

South-water-to-north Project , Natural-gas-from-the-west-to-the-east Project and Transmission of Electricity from the West to the East Project

The energy resources in China are unevenly distributed: the west has more natural gas and electricity than the east, while fresh water resource is much more in the south than the north. To remedy this situation, Chinese government, apart from developing new resources, has done large engineering projects like South-water-to-north Project , Natural-gas-from-the-west-to-the-east Project and Transmission of Electricity from the West to the East Project.

South-water-to-north Project

This project involves transmission from the upper, middle and lower ranges of the Yangtze River to the north. When the project is completed, the Yangtze, Yellow, Huaihe and Haihe rivers will be connected into a network, covering a larger part of the country. The size and difficulty of this engineering project, the quantity of water to be transmitted

◆ Flood Discharge from the Gates in the Dam of Danjiangkou Reservoir, Part of the Central Route in the South-water-to-north Project

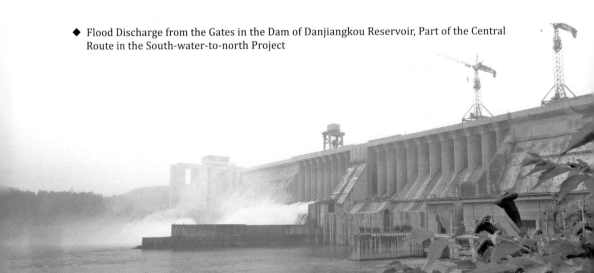

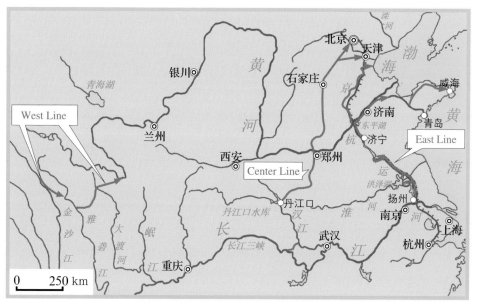

◆ The Map of South-water-to-north Project

and people to be benefited have been unprecedented in human history. So far, the completed first phase of the eastern route has benefited Jiangsu, Anhui, Shandong, Hebei and Tianjin with 14.3 billion cubic meters of fresh water. The conditions for Beijing are ready. The central route is being constructed, while the western route, yet to start. When all the three are completed in 2050, the quantity of water to be transmitted will be up to 44.8 billion cubic meters and people in the north will have water from the Yangtze River from taps.

To transmit water from the lower terrains in the south to the higher terrains in the north, pump stations in relay are a must, so the pump stations along the eastern route, the largest network in the world, is seen, able make water flow from lower to higher places. Technical innovations are many, like the super caliber PCCP pipe transmitting technology, pipe vehicles tunneling under the ground, barricade of super height, shallow-buried excavation and super caliber tunnels under pressure going under railways. These technologies are advancing in the world.

Natural-gas-from-the-west-to-the-east Project

In a newly completed residential neighborhood of Ningbo, Zhejiang Province, workers are doing safety check on natural gas pipes. If everything is fine, people can move into this neighborhood. Natural gas is as important to newly finished apartment buildings as other utilities like tap water and electricity.

Most households in big cities use natural gas to cook. People no longer rely on coal or replace old gas tank with a new one. Environments are improved. All this is possible by the natural gas from west to the east, a project beginning from 2002.

◆ The Tunnel Shield Work in Guangdong, Part of the Transport of Natural Gas from the West to the East Project

China's west is very rich in natural gas and oil resources, enough for the eastern part of China to use for dozens of years. So began the government's "transport of natural gas from the west to the east" project. Its second phase began to function in 2004. Its 40 thousand kilometers long pipe line went through 28 provinces to benefit over 400 million people. This project led in the world in many aspects, technology, equipment and materials used.

◆ The Tunnel Shield Work in Guangdong, Part of the Transport of Natural Gas from the West to the East Project

Transmission of Electricity from the West to the East Project

The southern part of China had the severest electricity shortage in history between 2004 and 2007, so came the Transmission of Electricity from the West to the East Project, a tremendous relief to the southern state grid. This project has proved very powerful, for during the severe sleet in early 2008, with the electricity from the west, the threat was reduced to minimum. In just a short while, power supply was back.

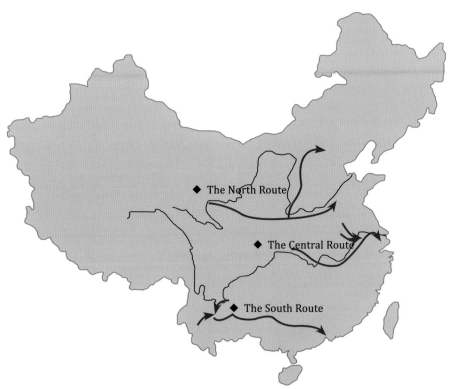

◆ The Map of Transmission of Electricity from the West to the East Project

◆ The Converter Station in Yulong, Sichuan Province

This project is to transmit badly needed electricity from the west to the east. Just in 2013, the 300 billion kilowatt-hour from Guizhou tremendously eased the power shortage in the fast progressing economy of the east.

So far, the Transmission of Electricity from the West to the East Project is not completed yet. In April 2013, an important part of it, the 2210-kilometer long from South Hami to Zhengzhou transmission project, the highest in voltage classes, biggest in transmission capacity and longest in distance worldwide, successfully crossed the Yellow River.

Qinghai-Tibet Railway, the Highest Railway Above the Sea Level in the World

The Qinghai-Tibet Plateau in China's southwest, the highest plateau in the world, has in it the Kunlun Mountains averagely 4000 meters above the sea level. It well deserves its nickname, "the roof of the world". This snow and ice bound plateau throughout a year challenges the bottom line for lives. Frozen earth, very thin air and lack of oxygen—just to name a few. Weather may go through spring to winter in a single day, brilliant sunny in the morning, hailstorms at noon time and minus 40 degrees Celsius at night.

"You want to make a fortune? Build a road first," Chinese people say. For ages, people tried but failed to connect the Qinghai-Tibet Plateau with inner land by a road. Paul Theroux, an American traveler, also a writer, wrote in his book, "Forget the idea of

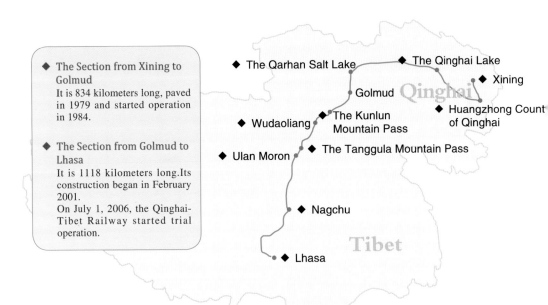

◆ The Section from Xining to Golmud
It is 834 kilometers long, paved in 1979 and started operation in 1984.

◆ The Section from Golmud to Lhasa
It is 1118 kilometers long.Its construction began in February 2001.
On July 1, 2006, the Qinghai-Tibet Railway started trial operation.

◆ The Qarhan Salt Lake
◆ The Qinghai Lake
◆ Xining
Golmud Qinghai
◆ Huangzhong Count of Qinghai
◆ Wudaoliang
◆ The Kunlun Mountain Pass
◆ Ulan Moron
◆ The Tanggula Mountain Pass
◆ Nagchu
Tibet
◆ Lhasa

◆ Sanchahe Bridge, the Highest Bridge Along the Qinghai-Tibet Railway

taking a railway ride to Lhasa, so long the Kunlun Mountains are there." This allegation became history when the Kunlun Mountain Tunnel, 1686 meters long and 4648 meters above the sea level, was completed as the longest one in the world through frozen earth on a plateau.

The Qinghai-Tibet Railway, the longest one on a plateau and also the highest above the sea level, was completed in July 2006. This 1952-kilometer long east-west railroad begins from Xining of Qinghai and ends at Lhasa of Tibet. People affectionately call it "the heaven road".

The difficulty in building this road was mountainous. Over a hundred thousand workers led an unbelievable hash life in this forbidding place, drinking bitter water from thawing snow, sleeping in tents and breathed in just 60 percent of oxygen at each breath. But they solved the toughest problems building a road in the harshest environments

Record-High Along the Qinghai-Tibet Railway

The highest plateau frozen earth tunnel above the sea level: the 1338-meter long Fenghuoshan Tunnel, 5100 meters above the sea level on top of the Fenghuoshan Mount.

The longest plateau frozen earth tunnel in the world: the Kunlun Mountain Tunnel, 1686 meters long and 4648 meters above the sea level.

The railway station highest above the sea level: Tanggula Station, 5068 meters above the sea level in Tanggula Mountain Pass.

The highest bridge on the Qinghai-Tibet Railway: Sanchahe Bridge, 690.19 meters long, 54.1 meters above the ground.

The longest road bridge on land: Qingshuihe Bridge, 11700 meters in length, 4500 meters above the sea level in Hoh Xil's no man's land.

like very fragile eco-system, high altitude, cold weather, lack of oxygen, perennial frozen earth and fierce wind... They made many "firsts" in the history of engineering. They initiated the practice of building a railroad on a bridge. This efficiently solved the unstable frozen soil layer, left routes open for wild animals to migrate and protected local eco-system.

The completion of the Qinghai-Tibet Railway ended the history of Tibet without a railroad. It improved the investment environment and boosted Tibetan economy. Local people have been tremendously benefited.

◆ Qinghai-Tibet Railway

The Largest High-speed Railway Network in the World

Chinese people used to have a difficult decision to make whenever they wanted to travel: train ride was inexpensive but too slow, while traveling by air, fast but too expensive. Now, they have another choice, inexpensive and still very fast, CRH.

CRH falls into two types: 200 kilometers per hour services headed with D, and 300 kilometers per hour services headed with G. By September 2013, the operation length of high-speed railways were up to 10 thousand kilometers in China, 45% of the world's total. It was very surprising that China mastered this technology in such a short time, and become the nation that has the longest mileage.

"Doubtlessly," the *New York Times* claimed in September 23, 2013, "CRH has changed China in a way never seen before!" Indeed, CRH has shortened the distance between cities, made itself the number one choice for travelers. Many people have preferred it to self-driving. From Dalian to Beijing, for instance, the gasoline cost for self driving is 500 Yuan (exclusive of road tolls) for a single trip. It took 8 hours to cover the distance if you were lucky enough not to get caught in a traffic jam. But, if you took the second-class D high-speed train, it cost only 260 Yuan and six hours to complete the trip. The advantages are obvious, faster, timesaving and environmental friendly.

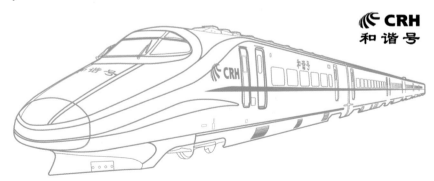

◆ The High-speed Train Service from Wuhan to Guangzhou

Data

The First Commercial Magnetic Levitation Train Service in Shanghai

The product of joint venture between China and Germany in January 2003, the train on this magnetic levitation line can go 430 kilometers per hour between Shanghai's Longyang and Pudong International Airport, taking just 8 minutes to cover the 30 kilometer distance, not much slower than the speed of an airplane. Magnetic levitation enables a train not to touch the rails while moving smoothly, comfortably and noise-free.

So far, China is working on another technology, vacuum duct magnetic levitation technology, which enables a train to move up to 4000 kilometers an hour, theoretically, close to the first cosmic velocity and it is extremely safe, consuming much less energy, producing very little noise and waste emission. Accident rate? Almost zero. Once this technology is put to use, it takes only two hours to travel from Beijing to Washington DC, and a couple of hours to go around the world.

◆ The Magnetic Levitation Train in Shanghai

The Three Gorges Power Project, the Largest Water Conservancy Engineering Work in the World

Since ancient times, in the middle and lower reaches of the Yangtze River has been a hanging river about 10 meters above the ground. If the dyke broke, Wuhan would be flooded. In 1931, a breach took 145 thousand lives. The threat was gone in 2009, when the Three Gorges Power Project was completed. In 2012, in the super floods the Yangtze River had ever seen, the project proved strong and effective, cutting the peak

◆ The Three Gorges Dam in Yichang, Hubei Province

◆ The Flood Discharge from the Three Gorges Dam
On July 20, 2010, the Three Gorges Power Project met the largest flood in history, 70 thousand cubic meters per second, breaking the record of 1998 in Yichang.

clipping by 40 percent. Huge tides, meters high close to the project, became submissive and peaceful before they continued to the lower reaches.

This project, so far the largest water conservancy project in the world, has three parts, the dam, the hydropower station and navigation structures. The power station is also the largest of its kind in the world, and by the end of 2012, its accumulative total capacity was up to 629.1 billion kilowatt-hour. The huge economic benefits of this project has been seen in other aspects like flood prevention, electricity generation and shipping. In construction size, science and technology and comprehensive utilization, the Three Gorges Power Project is a man-made wonder in human history.

Data

The Gezhou Dam, the First Hydropower Station on the Yangtze River

This dam is located in the lower reaches of the Yangtze River in Yichang, Hubei Province, 38 kilometers from the Three Gorges Power Project. The Gezhou Dam is the first large water conservancy project ever built on the Yangtze River, also the largest low water head mass flow hydroelectricity power station. Its construction began in December 1970 and was completed in December 1988. 12 by 12 meters large gates are built along its 2606.5 meters long dam, able to discharge 83.9 thousand cubic meters of water in maximum. This project was safe in the flood in July 1981, the largest flood over the past 100 years. Also, its single stage navigation lock was the largest, most advanced in technology and most sophisticated China ever built during the 20th century. It was an important passageway along the Yangtze River. The installed gross capacity was 2.715 million kilowatts, and for years running it has averagely generated 15.7 billion kilowatt-hour, saving coal by 10 million tons per year if compared with a thermal power station.

◆ Flood Discharge at Gezhou Dam